Davina Dupree
Cracks a
Christmas Code

S K Sheridan

Late Morning, Thursday, 22nd December

Yo, ho, ho, Diary!

I'm so excited, I can't believe there are only three more days until Christmas Day! Of course, I was a *bit* shocked when I heard I'd be staying at Egmont Exclusive Boarding School for the whole of the Christmas holidays, instead of going home with my old nanny Carrie like usual, but I suppose it's not her fault that she broke her ankle. It must have been a shock, falling off her step ladder like that, when all she was trying to do was put the star on top of the Christmas tree. I nearly choked on my salami and parmesan cheese pizza when I got her letter explaining it all. It's a good thing her friend Nora, who used to be a nurse, offered to take her in and look after her for a few weeks, otherwise I'd worry myself sick about how she was managing.

I have to say that my best friend Arabella has been absolutely brilliant about the whole thing. As soon as she heard that I was staying at school over Christmas, she rang up her parents and told them that she was staying here too! Can you believe it? So actually, I think these holidays are going to be pretty fun – although of course I'll miss Carrie. Bertie the gardener has decorated the corridors, dining hall and classrooms in a rather festive.com way; wreaths and garlands hang from the walls and ceilings, candles light up the darkest corners, holly and mistletoe are draped over everything possible, and Arabella says she saw him dragging the most ENORMOUS Christmas tree through the front door yesterday evening.

Some bad news, Diary: Cleo and Clarice, the two meanest girls in the whole school, are staying here as well. Apparently both sets of parents went skiing together last week, and yesterday their resort was covered by the biggest avalanche for thirty two years. Luckily everyone is ok as they were in bed at the time, but Cleo got a call from her mother saying the emergency services say it will be at least three weeks before anyone can leave the resort, so that means she and Clarice will be at Egmont for Christmas, like us. Oh well, we'll just have to make sure we keep out of their way.

Most of the other pupils went home last week. It did make me feel a bit strange, staring out of our dorm window, watching all the private jets and helicopters swoop down and pick up girls dressed in pink and white, before zooming off again. It's so QUIET.COM here now. At least there are a few of us left, as well as us and Cleo and Clarice, there's Simone from the second year, Becky and Teresa from the fourth year, and two sixth formers I don't know. Our lovely headmistress, Mrs Fairchild, is being an absolute lamb, of course, and says she's organised an exciting surprise for us girls for later on today, I can hardly wait to see what it is. Mrs F says that Christmas is her favourite time of year, and for the last few days she's been dressing up as a different festive character. On Monday she was wearing reindeer antlers made from felt, and had coloured her nose red. On Tuesday she was dressed as an angel and on Wednesday she was wearing an elf's costume! I can't wait to see what she's wearing today. Cleo and Clarice sneer behind their hands every time they see her dressed up, but I think Mrs F is really exciting to be around, you never know what she's going to do next.

Right, Diary, I've got to go now, as Arabella is shouting at me to come down to the kitchens. There's such a delish.com smell wafting around our dorm that she wants to see if Marcel the Chef has got lunch ready early today. Honestly, that girl does love food.

Just After Lunch, Thursday, 22nd December

Hmm, mysterious goings on, Diary.

Arabella made me hang around the kitchen for half an hour, watching Marcel's every move until lunch was ready. It was amazing, of course; mouth wateringly tender roast beef with roasted vegetables, garlic and herb roast potatoes and a yummy gravy.

Just as I was scraping the last bit of gravy off my plate, Mrs Fairchild twirled over with a pile of post in her hand. She was dressed as a Christmas cracker.

'Just being the Christmas post lady,' she giggled, and a letter fluttered down on to my lap.

I checked the handwriting – I always do this – to see who it was from, as the people I usually get letter from are my old nanny, Carrie Whepple, and my parents (who predictably can't come home this Christmas, as they are on a top secret mission somewhere in the North Pole). But I'd never seen this writing before in my life. Hmm, who could it be? Intrigued, I ripped the envelope open carefully, slipped out a beautiful Christmas card, that had a glittery Father Christmas riding on a sleigh stacked high with presents on the front.

'Who's it from?' Arabella asked, chewing. 'Carrie?'

'No, I don't think so,' I said.

I opened the card and read the message out loud:

"Dearest Davina,

This will be one cracker of a Christmas,

So stay alert, keen and wise.

Follow your heart, nose and clues

To find your festive surprise.

Lots of love....?"

There was a pause, while Arabella and I both took in the words.

'Wow,' Arabella said slowly, her mouth full. 'How mysterious. It sounds like someone's *giving* you a Christmas mystery to solve. Whoever it is must know you well enough to understand that solving mysteries is something you absolutely love doing.'

'I know,' I said. I read the card to myself three more times. 'But who could it be? Have you ever seen this handwriting before?' I leaned over and showed Arabella the card.

'Nope,' she said, munching. 'It's sort of wobbly, isn't it? Maybe from a child who can't write very well yet?'

'Hmm,' I said, feeling excited. 'My first hunch is that it's from Mrs Fairchild. Maybe it's a kind of thank you to both of us, because she knows you ALWAYS help solve the mysteries, for our detective work this year. She could have disguised her writing so we didn't think it was from her.'

'Let's go and ask her,' Arabella said, wiping her mouth. 'Come on, look- she's just twirling out of the dining room.'

We ran over.

'Mrs Fairchild,' I called. 'Wait for us.'

Our tiny headmistress stopped twirling and grinned.

'Sorry my pets,' she said. 'Always get a bit carried away, once you start spinning you just can't stop!'

'Mrs Fairchild,' I said, suddenly feeling a bit shy. 'I was just wondering if you know anything about this?' I held the card out, and she took it. 'Erm, actually, we were wondering if it was from you?'

Mrs Fairchild read the writing and gave a tinkly laugh.

'How exciting,' she said. 'But I'm afraid it has absolutely nothing to do with me, although I now wish it did. Look at the envelope it came in. It might have a postage mark, so you can see what area it was sent from.'

'Good idea,' Arabella said, while I rummaged through the pocket of my skirt and pulled out a rather crumpled envelope. I held it up to the light.

'There's a stamp that has print over it, but it's too smudged to make out any words.'

'Hey, what's that?' Arabella bent down and scooped up a tiny bit of paper in her hand. 'It fell when you unfolded the envelope.' She passed it to me. I opened it up and read it aloud.

'"*The first clue shall be found in a splashing zone, by a circle of life that is hung on its own*". Whatever does that mean?'

'I think I know,' Arabella said. 'The only splashing place around here is the swimming pool. I bet the first clue is somewhere in there.'

'But that will have to wait for later, my dears,' Mrs Fairchild allowed herself one more spin. 'Because it's nearly time for this afternoon's surprise to begin. Come on, there's good people, lead the way to the front lawn and I'll rally the rest of the troops. I have a feeling you're going to like this...'

Afternoon, Thusday, 22nd December

Wow, Diary!

When Arabella and I reached the front lawn, Cleo,

Clarice and the rest of the pupils were close behind us. Bertie the gardener was there too, a big grin on his old face, as well as Mrs Pumpernickle, wearing a floury apron – apparently she'd been making mince pies – and Marcel's niece, Adele, who's come to stay with him over Christmas.

Suddenly, a Christmas carol started playing through a hidden speaker, and Mrs Fairchild came scampering down the front steps.

'They're here, they're here,' she squealed, clapping her hands.

'Who?' Cleo said, sounding bored.

'The Brandy-Snaps, of course,' Mrs Fairchild said. 'They are a husband and wife team of animal trainers, and they've got your surprise. Look.'

We all looked, and saw a brown and white truck drive carefully down the long drive ahead of us. It came to a gentle halt near the patch of lawn we were standing on, and two people got out.

'Hello everyone,' the woman – who is VERY tall – said. 'Hello Mrs Fairchild, nice to see you again. Shall we unload?'

'Please do,' our headmistress winked. So the man, who is VERY short, winked back, and went round to the side of the truck. He unscrewed various bolts, then the whole of the brown and white side slid downwards, revealing four reindeer, standing calmly on a bed of straw.

'Reindeer!' Me and Arabella breathed together. I looked round, even Clarice and Cleo looked suitably impressed.

'This is your surprise girls,' Mrs Fairchild laughed her tinkly laugh. 'I know some of you would prefer to be with your families over Christmas but are having to stay at school due to personal circumstances, so I thought having some friendly reindeer to look after would take your mind off any of that, while at the same time getting you in the Christmas spirit. What do you all think?'

'Amazing,' Adele said in her French accent, going forward to stroke the nose of one of the reindeer. 'Incroyable. Ils sont magnifique.'

'What did she say?' Cleo said loudly.

'She said, "amazing, they are beautiful",' Simone said. She used to live in France when she was little, because her father was an ambassador there. I wish I could speak French, but the truth is I'm pretty shocking at it.

'I thought she was here to learn English,' Clarice said rudely. 'Why is she speaking French?'

'Perhaps you could learn some French from Adele, Clarice, then you wouldn't be bottom of the class all the time,' Arabella said loudly, her eyes flashing. She HATES it when Cleo and Clarice are rude to people; so do I but

I'm not as good at standing up to them as she is. I hope they don't all come to blows this holiday.

'The reindeer,' Mrs Fairchild said, completely ignoring the bickering. 'Are owned by this lovely couple, Mr and Mrs Brandy-Snap. These kind people have agreed to stay in one of the guest cottages at the edge of the grounds over Christmas, to be on hand to look after the reindeer but also to train you lot to look after them.'

'Wow,' I said, going over to the truck too and stroking the soft nose of a reindeer. It felt like crushed velvet and I immediately fell in love with all four animals. 'Thanks so much for arranging this, Mrs Fairchild. What a treat!'

Mrs Fairchild twirled away, saying she was going to be late for her kick-boxing class, so me, Arabella and the rest of the girls stayed on the lawn for TWO more happy hours, getting to know both the reindeer and the Brandy-Snaps. The Brandy-Snaps are super; really friendly and kind. They said their plan is to let the reindeer graze wherever they want around the school grounds – the cattle grids further up the drive will prevent them from escaping - and the animals are so tame they won't mind us going and stroking them whenever we want. EXTREMELY excitingly unusual.com, don't you think?

Anyway Diary, I MUST go and search the swimming pool for the first clue with Arabella. I've been racking my brain all day but still can't imagine who the card's from, although I'm thinking maybe one of our friends like Melody or Lottie, who've gone home for Christmas – perhaps they wanted to give us a nice surprise or something? Anyway, we've got to be quick because in half an hour a local lady from Little Pineham is coming in to give us an art and craft lesson – we're going to learn how to make Christmas wreaths! Off to the "splashing zone" we hurry...

Late Afternoon, Thursday, 22nd December

We found the next clue, Diary!

Basically, Arabella and I literally SPRINTED over to the

swimming pool, just before it was time for wreath making. We had to cover our heads with our arms as we weren't wearing coats and it had started to drizzle. It was also FREEZING – I wonder if it's going to snow?

Anyway, when we got there, the warm dampness inside the pool area dried us pretty quickly.

We looked around, up at the colourful shoots and slides that twirl through the air above the crystal clear water.

'Hmm,' I said. 'I hope the next clue's not hidden in one of those shoots, Arabella. We don't have our swimming costumes and there's not enough time to run back and get them.'

'No, I don't think it will be. Remember what the words on that bit of paper were: "The first clue shall be found in a splashing zone, by a circle of life that is hung on its own". What could they mean by a circle of life? Oh no, look who it is.'

I peered towards the water and saw two jewelled swimming hats bobbing towards us. A sneering face stared out from beneath each.

'Oh look, it's the nerdy wannabe detectives,' Clarice sniggered. 'What are you doing, girls? Looking for another silly little mystery to solve?'

'Or perhaps you're both too shy to put your plain old swimming costumes on?' Cleo said, winking at her friend.

'Mine's new, Mummy sent it last week. It's made from gold thread and has real diamonds round the neck.'

'Sounds itchy,' Arabella said. 'Can't stand that sort of thing myself. Come on, Davina, I'm getting a headache standing here.'

We turned and walked as far away from them as we could, ignoring the cackles of laughter behind us. When we'd reached the other side of the pool, and could no longer hear their screechy voices, I leant back against the wall.

'I wish those two weren't staying here over Christmas,' I said, feeling rather glum.com. 'They're always so rude.'

'Just ignore them,' Arabella said. Her cheeks had gone bright red so I knew she was annoyed. 'They're not worth even thinking about.'

'Hey, what about this?' I said, turning to stare at the object next to me. It was a shiny red and white ring. 'You're supposed to throw this to struggling swimmers, aren't you? Maybe this would fit the description, "circle of life"?'

'Ooh, good idea,' Arabella said, cheering up. 'Let's examine it.'

We examined every inch of the life ring, running our fingers across the front and back, looking at the rope that framed it, even trying to *see* behind it, which was difficult as it was jammed quite close to the wall. Just as I was feeling rather stumped, I ran my fingers all around the hook that took its weight.

'Ooh, what's this?' I retrieved a tiny square of folded paper, quickly undoing it. 'I've found it, Arabella! Listen to this: *"You've found me, well fancy that! Next, an equine creature's looking after a hat"*. What does equine mean?'

'I'm not sure, we can look it up,' Arabella rolled up her sleeve and stared at her watch. 'But it will have to be later, we should have been at the wreath making workshop three minutes ago.'

'Right,' I grinned, feeling excited. 'These holidays are turning out to be pretty fun, aren't they?'

We had SUCH fun at the wreath making workshop, my fingers smelt all pine-needly for ages afterwards. I've hung my wreath - which has red dried herbs and flowers woven throughout it and a big red and green tartan bow at the bottom – on our dorm door. Arabella gave hers to Marcel to hang on the kitchen door.

Right, Diary. Arabella and I are quickly going to look up "equine" in the dictionary before dinner...

Evening, Thursday, 22nd December

Diary!

"Equine" means horse! Now we know EXACTLY where to

look for the next clue – in the school stables. The only problem is that because it's winter we're not allowed out after dark, and believe me it's *very* dark and cold outside at the moment. We're planning to search the stables first thing tomorrow morning.

Dinner was another triumph by Marcel and his team of chefs; Beef Wellington in yummy flaky pastry, with spicy red cabbage for the side and cinnamon bread and butter pudding for dessert. Yumsters! In fact I ate so much, it's made me rather sleepy...Zzzzzzzz

Morning, Friday, 23rd December

Discoveries and an announcement, Diary!

So, of course we headed STRAIGHT to the stables after breakfast. Arabella read out the other clue again, "You've found me, well fancy that! Next, an equine creature's looking after a hat", and we went to the shelf where the riding hats are stored, in the tack room.

All the girls at Egmont have their own riding hats, with silky patterned material called 'silks' stretched over the top. My silks are turquoise with deep purple flowers all round the rim, and Arabella's are black and white zigzags. We eventually found our hats in the brightly coloured pile, then began the search for the next clue, looking inside the hats and beneath the silks. We literally checked every centimetre of our hats but didn't find another clue anywhere.

'What did the clue at the swimming pool say again?' Arabella asked, throwing her hat back onto the pile.'

'You've found me, well fancy that! Next, an equine creature's looking after a hat,' I replied, throwing mine back on the shelf slightly harder than necessary.

'An equine creature's looking after A hat, not necessarily yours or mine,' Arabella said. 'It could be in ANY hat in this stable. It's going to take AGES to find.'

'Right, you start looking through the others in this pile, I'll take a walk round the stable looking for more hats that aren't on the shelf,' I said, feeling worried. I still didn't know who'd given me this Christmas mystery to solve but all I knew was that I was enjoying it, and didn't want it to stop, just because we couldn't find a clue.

I walked slowly around the tack room, where all the horsy equipment is kept. Egmont's tack room has baby pink walls with silver pegs in rows all over them. There are deep purple shelves everywhere, for different sets of equipment, and a few higher gold pegs for the teacher's hats.

I ran my fingers round every shelf and object I

encountered, my eyes searching for any folded bit of paper, and crack it could have been stuffed into.

Just when my heart was feeling really flat, and I'd examined nearly every inch of the room, my eyes rested on the one hat I'd never thought to look at. High up, on the biggest gold peg in the room, hung Mrs Fairchild's riding hat. I've always thought it looks like a work of art, because whoever designed it managed to make the top layer from a soily substance that plants can grow in, so throughout the year Mrs F's hat is covered in real, beautiful seasonal flowers.

I carefully took it down and inspected the flowers. A petally perfume whooshed right up my nose, at the same time as I noticed a tiny scroll resting in the centre of a scarlet orchid.

'Arabella,' I yelled. 'I think I've found it!'

She arrived beside me in seconds, and I read out the new clue:

"'*Well done, you're doing well. Now follow your stomachs and that delicious smell*". What smell?' I asked, sniffing.

'Ah, this is my area of expertise,' Arabella grabbed my hand and pulled me outside into the crisp winter air. A pale gold sun shone through the white sky, making the grounds sparkle beautifully.

'*Now* sniff,' she said, grinning.

As I sniffed the air and took in the delicious aroma of freshly baking bread, a reindeer wandered over. I stroked his nose and cuddled his neck, and the reindeer seemed to be sniffing the air too.

'He can smell the bread,' Arabella laughed. 'Marcel and his chefs always make batches of bread at this time in the morning – haven't you noticed before?'

'No, there are always different delicious smells coming out of the kitchen, I've never realised they happen at certain times of day,' I grinned. 'But how did our mystery person know we'd find this clue just at the time when Marcel was baking bread?'

'They didn't!' Arabella said, giving the reindeer a stroke. 'Like you just said, there are always yummy smells coming out of the kitchen, whatever the time of day. So they knew they'd be safe to say "follow your stomachs and that delicious smell"!'

We went to the kitchens after saying goodbye to the reindeer, but Marcel was in a complete flap because one of the trainee chefs had just dropped a jug on the floor and it had shattered, so there was the usual chef drama about cleaning up the mess.

''E 'as RUINED eet,' Marcel cried, as we pushed open the kitchen door. 'Just look at ze floor, CARNAGE. That's eet, my day eez over, I may as well go back to BED!'

'Er, would it be ok if we came and looked around the kitchen for a few minutes,' Arabella said, quite bravely in my opinion. 'It's just that –'

'No it would NOT,' Marcel shouted. 'Can't you see a crisis 'as occurred?'

'Ok, sorry to bother you Marcel, we'll come back later,' I said, taking Arabella's hand and dragging her out before she said anything else.

Just as we were heading down the corridor, enjoying the feel of the squashy carpet beneath our feet, one of the fourth years, Becky, came round the corner.

'Have you heard?' She asked, as she came nearer.

'What?' We both said together.

'Mrs Pumpernickle's asked us to all meet in the hall after lunch,' Becky said in her brisk way. 'We're going to perform a carol concert at Little Pineham's Elderly Care Home for all the residents on Christmas Morning, so we have to start practising. Apparently there's a fashion designer coming in tomorrow to help us make Christmassy outfits for the show.'

'Cool,' Arabella breathed, and I grinned at the thought – art is my absolute favourite subject, so making Christmassy outfits with a fashion designer sounded amazing.com.

'We'll have to sneak into the kitchen after carol practise,'

Arabella whispered, as Becky disappeared down the corridor. 'We don't want the clue trail to go cold!'

Afternoon, Friday, 23rd December

What a day, Diary.

After a delish.com lunch of roasted asparagus, spiced chicken and zesty ice cream, Arabella and I made our way to the hall. The sound of scales being thrashed out on the grand piano met our ears before we'd even turned the door handle.

A Christmassy scene greeted us: Bertie the gardener, who is actually excellent at the piano – Mrs F said he used to be a semi-professional musician before he took up landscape gardening - was wearing a Santa hat and sitting on the piano stool, his hands pumping up and down across the keys. The enormous Christmas tree that Arabella saw Bertie dragging through the front door the other day stood proudly in a large gold pot at the back of the stage, ten large boxes of Christmas decorations next to it. Cleo and Clarice were slumped in front row seats, filing their nails, Mrs F was twirling across the stage dressed as a snowman. Mrs Pumpernickle was standing eating a mince pie, Adele was humming, and Becky, Simone and Teresa stood near Mrs Pumpernickle, looking at song sheets. The sixth formers were nowhere to be seen.

I set off towards the stage, Arabella close behind me, and as we arrived next to Mrs Pumpernickle the door swung open and the three important looking sixth formers strode in, soon joining us.

Mrs F stopped twirling and clapped her hands together.

'We're all here, how thrilling,' she tinkled. 'Bertie, do stop playing for a minute, there's a lamb, I just want to explain to the girls what's going on.'

Bertie stopped and wiped the beads of sweat from his brow.

'Now,' Mrs Pumpernickle said as she handed out song

sheets to us new arrivals. 'As some of you know, it's an Egmont custom to perform a carol concert at Little Pineham's Elderly Care Home on Christmas morning. It's a lovely affair and the old dears are *so* grateful, they usually give us a slap up feast of mince pies, Christmas cake and spiced fizzy apple juice afterwards.' She looked towards Cleo and Clarice. 'Are you going to come up here and join us, girls?'

'But carol singing is so *boring*,' Clarice groaned, staggering to her feet. 'And we're missing the next episode of Gossiping Shoppers.'

'Yeah,' Cleo tucked her nail file behind her ear and stood up. 'Now we'll never find out what

Patsy said to Maisy after Daisy said she didn't like spaghetti.'

'How awful for you,' Mrs F said seriously. 'Oh well, why not try and do this for the elderly people, if not for yourselves? Christmas is a time of giving, after all.'

'And receiving,' Cleo nudged Clarice and they both sniggered. Arabella rolled her eyes.

Minutes later, we were all belting out Christmas carols, with Mrs F conducting. Simone and Teresa have lovely singing voices and Adele surprised us by singing harmonies over the top of our carols, and to be honest I thought we sounded pretty good! Bertie played away, sweat pouring down his head; he's really rather good at the piano.

Just when my throat was starting to hurt from all the singing, Mrs F clapped her hands together and said,

'Oh well done, my darlings. A brilliant effort all round. I think we'll stop there, and have one more practise tomorrow morning. Remember, a fashion designer will be arriving tomorrow afternoon to help you make festive costumes for the concert – I can't wait to see what you come up with. Now, who wants to help me decorate the Christmas tree?'

We all put up our hands, even Adele and the sixth formers.

'Lovely, let's get cracking,' Mrs F said, turning to dig into the first box of decorations.

Mrs Pumpernickle handed round mince pies and glasses of ginger beer as we decorated the tree, while Bertie played carols softly on the grand piano. I felt so festive by the time we'd finished, I almost felt it was Christmas day already.

'Let's stand back and admire our masterpiece,' Mrs F said, taking a few steps backwards. We all did the same and I have to say I was impressed by the result. The tall tree was decorated from top to bottom with sparkling decorations – miniature sledges, reindeer, snowmen, bells, presents, wreaths, candles, stars, mistletoe and stockings hung from the sweet smelling branches. Bertie stopped playing the piano long enough to light the real candles that perched on several branches – the sixth formers had decorated the highest parts of the tree – and when they were all alight we gasped in appreciation. The tree really did look Christmas card perfect.

'Amazing, you clever things,' Mrs F said fondly, looking round at all of us. 'Now go and pet the reindeer, they must have been wondering where you've all got to. Don't forget your coats, hats and scarves; the weathers getting colder by the minute.'

So that's where Arabella and I are off to now, Diary – we just popped back to our dorm to get our warm winter coats. Finding the next clue in the kitchen will have to wait till this evening...

Evening, Friday, 23rd December

The mystery deepens, Diary...

After a good hour of reindeer petting – they really are the most gorgeous.com creatures, the way they like having their antlers rubbed – Arabella and I slipped away to the kitchen. We were following our stomachs as we were rather hungry, and there was certainly a delish smell wafting out of the steamy room, and when we arrived the earlier crisis had clearly been dealt with and forgotten because all the chefs were slapping Marcel on the back and congratulating him on producing the "finest truffle sauce they 'ad ever tasted".

'Ahem, could we pop in and have a look around, Marcel?' Arabella called from the door. 'We're really sorry to interrupt as we know you're cooking dinner, but we think something we need is hidden in here.'

'Ah, come in, come in,' Marcel turned, beaming from ear to ear. 'We are not only cooking, we are celebrating, mon Cherie. I 'ave just created the finest, most exquisite sauce in the universe, come – try it.'

We both went over and stared at the mysterious, thick,

golden liquid in question. It filled a silver jug, which the chefs were staring at lovingly. Marcel found two spoons, filled them and passed them to us.

'Let ze ingredients – ze rich black truffle shavings, ze fluffy eggs, ze finest mustard grains, ze lemon zest, ze secret 'erb mix and ze olive oil, sit on your tongues for a minute so you can understand the full magnificence of this accomplishment,' Marcel was quivering with excitement as he awaited our responses.

I did as he said, sliding the golden sauce on to my tongue and leaving it there. A taste explosion immediately went off in my mouth, layers of nuttiness, tanginess and herbiness with a

hint of mushroom zooming
around everywhere.

'Wow,' I said, swallowing it.
'Seriously, Marcel, that's
absolutely fantastic.'

'More,' Arabella said,
looking greedily at the jug as she
licked her spoon. 'More please
Marcel.'

'Ah mon little treasures, I
am glad you like ze sauce,' he
patted our heads affectionately.
'But you will 'ave to wait for ze
dinner, which is in 'alf an hour, to
'ave any more. Now you can
search the kitchen for whatever it
eez, just stay out of our way,
merci.'

We left the huddle of chefs
and began exploring the silver
and white, extremely clean

kitchen. Marcel liked everything EXACTLY in its place and the rows of utensils were lined up in neat lines, saucepans in size order, pots neatly labelled with his fancy writing, sieves, ladles, spatulas and other mysteriously shiny objects hanging in tidy rows from the ceiling. We searched behind everything we could reach, but found nothing.

'What are you looking for?' Marcel said as he zoomed past, holding a tray of crackling pork high in the air.

'A tiny bit of paper,' Arabella said glumly, clearly feeling it was going to be difficult to find here.

'Ah Cherie, the only paper we 'ave in 'ere is in our recipe

books,' Marcel said as he zoomed back again.

'Right,' I said, looking around. 'Now that sounds more hopeful.'

We spotted the books on three high shelves to the right of the kitchen, and managed to reach them by standing on shiny metal stools. Arabella slid the one nearest her out and opened it, flicking through page after page about mouth-wateringly good cakes. I slid one out about different types of gravy, but just as I was about to open it Arabella shouted –

'Found it!'

She quickly unfolded the now familiar square of paper and read out the words:

'"Good work, now think of
spades in barrels, the owner of
these likes Christmas carols".
Spades in barrels? What on earth
are those?'

'I don't know,' I said, at the
same time as Marcel cried,

'Dinner's ready!'

I ate so much pork and
truffle sauce I can hardly move –
in fact I think I need to lie down
for a bit now, Diary. Me and
Arabella will turn our attention to
spades in barrels – whatever they
may be – in the morning. Good
night xx

**Christmas Eve Morning,
Saturday, 24th December**

Jingle Bells, Diary.

No seriously, I can hear Jingle Bells playing in the corridor outside our dorm, Mrs Pumpernickle has hired a brass band from the local village, and they are patrolling the corridors playing carols and Christmas songs very loudly on trumpets, trombones, saxophones and French horns. Super festive.com.

After Arabella and I had eaten a slap up breakfast of bacon, eggs, sausages and toast, while watching Mrs Fairchild – who is dressed as a Christmas stocking today – dance around the room, we turned our attention to what the clue might mean.

'What did it say again?' I asked, wiping my mouth with my napkin.

'I think it said, "Good work, now think of spades in barrels, the owner of these likes Christmas carols"', Arabella said. I noticed that her cheeks were bright red. 'I think the heating's on too high,' I said, feeling rather flushed myself all of a sudden. 'Shall we go for a walk around the grounds to cool off? The morning air might help us think.'

'Good idea,' Arabella said, and very soon we were strolling arm in arm, wearing our thickest coats, out of the front door and over to a reindeer who was grazing a few feet away.

'Hello there,' I said, rubbing its antlers. 'Can you help us, reindeer? What do you think the clue means?' The animal just snorted in reply.

'Hey look, there's Bertie,' Arabella said, patting the reindeer's back. 'Surely he can't be putting *more* Christmas decorations up? The schools already full of them.'

We watched as Bertie pushed his wheelbarrow – full of berries, holly and mistletoe - round the side of the school, soon disappearing out of view.

'Hey!' Arabella shouted suddenly. She grabbed my arm and pulled. 'I've got an idea.'

Seconds later I found myself being dragged towards Bertie's shed. The door stood ajar and Arabella swung it wide open.

'As I watched him go round the corner, I remembered where I've seen barrels recently,' she grinned. 'Bertie likes them because they're so big he can store lots of his tools in them. Look, there's a barrel full of rakes, one full of garden shears and one full of spades.'

'Well done,' I grinned back. 'But what about the Christmas carol bit?'

'That fits too,' Arabella said, going over to the barrel full of spades. 'Bertie was playing the accompaniment for our carols the other evening, he's a pretty good musician actually, and he'll be there at the concert practise today. I think he loves Christmas carols, he was whistling one just now when he was pushing the wheelbarrow.'

This time the clue was easy to find. We both spotted it at the same time, balanced on the top of a rusty spade at the back of the barrel. I grabbed it and unfolded it.

'"Where paints and pastels lie side by side, you'll find another clue by the colour tide". Hmm, sounds like the art room, don't you think?'

'Yes, that's what I was thinking,' Arabella said. 'But we're going to have to go there later, the carol concert practise starts in five minutes.'

Christmas Eve, Early Evening, Saturday, 24th December

Things are getting more and more exciting.com, Diary...

We had a good carol practise this morning, the harmonies sound fab. The only slightly annoying thing was when Cleo and Clarice kept checking their phones when they were supposed to be singing; it got so bad that Mrs F asked Mrs Pumpernickle to confiscate the phones until after the practise – cue loud groans from Cleo and Clarice.

After a delish lunch of pate, cranberry chutney and different crackers from different countries around the world, me, Arabella and the rest of the pupils went to the hall to meet the fashion designer who'd come to help us make costumes to wear for the carol concert tomorrow at Little Pineham Elderly Care Home.

I gasped in delight as I walked into the hall and saw boxes of silky, flowing materials, tables laid out with arts and crafts, and a wicker basket full of the Christmassy plants we'd seen Bertie wheeling around in the morning. There was another table full of card, paper, glue, scissors, beads, sequins, glitter and lots of other arty accessories. Pure heaven!

Arabella looked at me and grinned. I knew she'd much rather do a maths problem than art, but she could see how happy this activity made me.

The fashion designer, a young woman called Nicola Nutmeg who was petite with bright white hair cut in a sharp bob and was wearing an a striking black and white trouser suit, said she was usually busy putting on fashion shows in Paris, London, Milan, New York, Tokyo, Madrid and Sydney, but happened to have a few days off so was happy to accept her old headmistress's invitation to come and teach costume design for an afternoon. Nicola used to be an Egmont pupil herself once – fancy that.com!

Anyway, it wasn't long before we were stuck into creating our own Christmassy outfits. Nicola showed us how to make accessories like hats, scarfs, bracelets, necklaces and hairbands out of felt, sequins and glitter. I made a red Christmas hat with a white, glittery rim, two bracelets from small, green felt holly leaves, a scarf made from white silk and a pair of red, green and white leg warmers which I decorated with images of stars, holly and robins. Arabella was very proud of herself because she made a really lovely bobble hat from gold and white felt, with tiny glittery snowflakes all over the gold rim. Then she made a matching scarf to match. Considering she doesn't usually like art and craft activities she did REALLY well at this one.

Of course Cleo and Clarice kept walking past our table being rude about our designs until Mrs Pumpernickle, who was drinking spiced apple juice out of a flask in the corner, told them that if they didn't sit down and stop being rude that instant they'd find themselves out in the cold air before you could say Merry Christmas.

When we'd finished our designs and had stopped admiring them, Arabella leaned over to whisper in my ear.

'Shall we slip away to the art room now and try and find the next clue?'

'Good idea,' I whispered back, and minutes later we were padding down the soft carpeted corridors towards my most favourite classroom in the whole school.

It was strange opening the door of the art room when

nobody else was around. Usually, when we have lessons there, there are girls milling around in the corridor, and teachers going in and out of different rooms. But in the holidays, parts of the school took on a deserted feel – and the art room was definitely one of these places. I almost felt as though we were trespassing as we crept into the large room and turned on the lights – it was already pretty dark outside.

We split up and started searching through the rows of paint bottles, boxes of pastels, pencils and pens, stores of brushes and palettes and boxes and rolls of brightly coloured fabrics.

'Hmm, the clue said something like, "Where paints

and pastels lie side by side, you'll find another clue by the colour tide", didn't it?' I called, from the opposite side of the art room to Arabella.

'Yep,' she called back, rummaging through a packet of glue sticks. 'But there's so much colour in here it will be like trying to find a needle in a haystack.'

'Hang on a minute,' I said, a thought occurring to me. I walked over to the big sink that had faint splashes of dried paint around its rim. 'I'm just going to check round here, because whenever I wash paint out of a palette it creates a rainbow tide in the sink.'

Almost as soon as I'd said the words, I caught sight of a

small folded piece of paper resting behind one of the taps.

'Aha,' I said, opening it quickly. 'Found it!'

Arabella came galloping across the room.

'What does it say?' She asked.

'"You're nearly there, so stop and think where gentle creature's yawn. The best time for this, I have to say, is at the crack of dawn". Well! Whatever does that mean?' I said, feeling puzzled.

'Hmm,' Arabella scratched her head. 'I think this is the most difficult one yet. And my stomach's telling me that if I don't feed it soon, I'll never have the brain power to work out the clue at all!'

'We'd better go and have some dinner in that case,' I grinned, realising how hungry I'd also become. 'Come on, I bet Marcel's cooked an extra especially nice one seeing as its Christmas Eve.'

Late Night, Christmas Eve, Saturday, 24th December

Diary!

You'll never guess what — we've had such an amazing evening with a rather unexpected surprise at the end of it. I know it's late and I should be going to sleep, but I just HAVE to write in you first.

After a slap up meal that started with canopies in Christmas cracker shapes, followed by chestnut and stilton pie with asparagus and courgette parcels and icing sugar croissants to finish, not to mention the fizzy cranberry and orange juice drinks - absolute yumsters.com – Mrs Fairchild, who was dressed as a snowflake, stood up and clapped her hands together. This wasn't really necessary as there are hardly any of us left in the school, but I think she's so used to doing it she did it anyway.

'And now,' she said, beaming round. 'It's time to hang up the stockings! Follow me, everyone.'

We all trooped after her, even the sixth formers, Mrs

Pumpernickle, Adele, Marcel and all the chefs. Mrs F led us to her own private drawing room which is attached to her study – a room most of us have been in at one time or other but which is usually out of bounds for casual visits – and the sight that met us made me grin from ear to ear.

A cosy fire crackled in the grate, the smell of freshly baked mince pies wafted through the air- I could see them cooling on a plate on a side table, the squashy sofas were placed in a nice sociable arrangement, and best of all – there were several large, knitted stockings laid out on a large oak table.

'Come in, come in,' Mrs Fairchild said. 'Choose your stocking and come over here.'

She went towards the fireplace and I now saw that there was a row of hooks in the stone mantelpiece. 'Hang it up on one of these – the mantelpiece is so wide they won't go anywhere near the fire so don't worry – and Father Christmas will no doubt arrive at some point this evening and fill it up! I haven't seen him for ages, knew his mother – lovely lady.'

I chose a red and white stocking with a robin embroidered on the front and Arabella chose a red, black and green one with holly leaves sewn round the rim. Soon, all the stockings were hung up, looking gorgeous all in a line, and we were sitting on the sofas tucking into mince pies galore. When everyone else was busy chatting and munching, I leaned towards Arabella and whispered,

'So what do you think, "You're nearly there, so stop and think where gentle creature's yawn. The best time for this, I have to say, is at the crack of dawn" actually means?'

'I'm not sure,' Arabella yawned herself. 'But I bet it's got something to do with the reindeer. They're the only gentle creatures I can think of round here. And we won't be able to get to see them till tomorrow morning at the earliest – the school is completely locked up now.'

'May I have your attention for one minute, my dears,' Mrs Fairchild beamed round before I could reply, as she wiped a mince pie crumb away from the corner of her mouth. 'Now, as you all know, we're performing our carol concert at Little Pineham Elderly Care Home at ten o'clock tomorrow morning. That means we have to assemble in the front hall at nine o'clock sharp so that Bertie can drive us all together in the platinum mini bus. I know Marcel will have presented you with an outstanding Christmas breakfast before that.' She winked at Marcel, who grinned back and said,

'Ah, it will be my pleasure, ma Cherie.'

'The wonderful Christmas costumes you all created with Nicola Nutmeg today will be laid out on a table in the entrance hall tomorrow morning, so please do collect them after breakfast and put them on for our performance – they will add the final touch to our Christmassy show,' Mrs Fairchild clapped her hands together and giggled. 'Honestly, this is all *too* exciting. You may use my drawing room as your own from the moment you wake up tomorrow to the moment you go to bed, so come and check your stockings any time. Now, away to your beds my little ones, and remember that Father Christmas prefers you to all be asleep when he arrives. It's just easier that way, after all he has *such* a busy schedule on Christmas Eve.'

So we went back to our dorms and I'm sure Arabella fell asleep even before her head touched her pillow. But I was too full of excitement and questions, and lay there for ages, wondering who on earth had sent me all those wonderful clues. Could it be a friend from Egmont, who'd gone home for the holidays? Possibly, but I didn't think so, somehow. I was sure it couldn't be my old nanny Carrie Whepple, the writing wasn't anything like hers and she'd broken her ankle so couldn't walk anywhere. Mrs Fairchild said it wasn't herself, but could it be someone else left at the school? Certainly not Cleo or Clarice, and I didn't really know the other girls well enough. Maybe even Arabella herself – could this all be an elaborate Christmas present from my best friend? But Arabella seemed genuinely puzzled by each clue. Could it be one of the new arrivals at Egmont, like Marcel's niece Adele, or the reindeers' owners, Mr and Mrs Brandy-Snap? But why would they go to all that trouble, when they hardly knew me. It really was too puzzling for words.

As I lay there, with thoughts whizzing round my head, listening to Church bells strike midnight, I heard another set of bells start ringing. They sounded high overhead, a sort of fizzy, jingly ringing sound, and through the crack in the curtains I saw a brilliant red streak fly through the night sky. Minutes later, hooves clattered on the cobbles outside and I heard a voice, that sounded like Mrs Fairchild's, exclaim,

'You made it! How lovely to see you. Gosh has it really been a whole year? Now do come and have a glass of sherry and a mince pie, you must be ravenous.'

Surely that couldn't be...Father Christmas?

I'm so tired now, Diary, I simply HAVE to go to sleep, but I can't wait for tomorrow morning and all the surprises that will bring!

Early Morning, Christmas Day, Sunday, 25th December

Merry Christmas, Diary!

Blimey, what a morning we've had already. Arabella woke

up first and literally JUMPED on me in excitement, and we tumbled off to Mrs Fairchild's drawing room pretty quickly.

The stockings hung in a row, bulging at the seams with exciting lumps and bumps sticking mysteriously out of each one.

'Father Christmas has been!' Arabella yelled at the top of her lungs, as she took down her stocking and delved into it. I did the same, and Arabella's voice seemed to have woken everyone else up as they arrived slowly after that, either individually or in pairs.

Mrs Fairchild walked in, wearing a bright pink onesie, with rollers in her hair.

'Merry Christmas, everybody,' she said, looking genuinely delighted to find us examining our stockings. Even Cleo and Clarice were being nicer than normal, and didn't say one mean thing to us – they were too busy inspecting their gifts.

At the top of my stocking, I found a chocolate sculpture, two girls with their arms round each other, wearing the Egmont pink and white uniform. On closer inspection, I saw that the two girls were me and Arabella! Underneath that was a digital bookmark, I've always wanted one of them, you can look anything up that you don't understand when you're reading or writing. Then there was a pack of fizzy bath bombs, a luxury art set, a digital photo frame, pens and pencils in every colour you can imagine, a miniature model of the whole of Egmont school – the detail is utterly amazing, and several books I haven't read. Yippee! Thank you Father Christmas, you got it just right, as always.

Arabella seemed extremely pleased with her gifts, which all seemed to have something to do with maths or science. We took our stockings and gifts back to our down and after examining them even more, went down for a mouth wateringly good Christmas breakfast. Marcel and his chefs had laid out a brekkie feast – lobster and caviar muffins, smoked salmon and watercress bagels, honey and cheese crumpets, apricot pancakes, cranberry porridge and bowls of blueberries, strawberries, blackberries and raspberries. Marcel and the chefs ate with us for once, which was really nice, everyone was in such a good mood lots of laughing and loud conversations filled the air, and Mrs Fairchild got a round of applause when she appeared wearing a Father Christmas outfit.

'I'm *Mother* Christmas,' she announced, to more applause.

'Let's grab our Christmas costumes from the hall and then head to the reindeer shed,' Arabella said, wiping her mouth with a Christmassy napkin. 'Phew, I've eaten so much I don't think I need to eat for at least a week!'

'Me too,' I said, grinning. 'Come on then, let's go.'

Afternoon, Christmas Day, Sunday, 25th December

A crisis, a solution and a big surprise, Diary!

A few minutes later we were in the large entrance hall, heading towards the table where the colourful outfits and accessories were laid out.

'There's Teresa's one,' Arabella said, pointing to a Father Christmas hat and snowflake earrings. 'And those three belong to Becky, Cleo and Clarice. I think those ones belong to the sixth formers, and I'm sure Adele made the one with the colourful pom poms all over the scarf. Simone made the gold scarf and glove set, but where are ours?'

'Erm,' I said, scratching my head, feeling really rather puzzled. 'We didn't take them up to our dorm, did we?'

'No we gave them to Nicola Nutmeg at the end,' Arabella said. 'Don't you remember, she went round collecting everybody's outfits at the end of the art and craft session.'

'Oh yes,' I said at the same time as Cleo and Clarice came swishing into the entrance hall, arms linked together.

'Hello nerd brains,' Clarice said. I didn't like the way she grinned at us. 'Looking for something?'

'We can't find out Christmassy costumes for the carol concert,' Arabella said, narrowing her eyes at them. 'You know something about where they are, don't you?'

'Oh well, we know how much you both love solving silly little mysteries,' Cleo's eyes gleamed unkindly. 'So we thought we'd create one for you, call it a Christmas present from us to you.'

'We've hidden your Christmas outfits,' Clarice said, as both mine and Arabella's mouths fell open at exactly the same time. 'If you can find them, you'll be able to come to the carol concert. If not, you'll just have to miss it. Let's see how good your detecting skills really are. And don't bother going to find Mrs Fairchild or Mrs Pumpernickle to whinge about us, they've already left for Little Pineham Care Home to set up for the concert. Bertie the gardeners in charge. Good bye girls, enjoy the hunt.'

They sniggered and sashayed off.

'The beasts!' I said loudly, feeling my cheeks burn hot with rage. 'I can't believe they've done this to us on Christmas day. *And* I thought they were being nicer than normal this morning.'

'Well they're making up for that now, that's for sure,' Arabella said grimly. 'Come on, let's go and find our stuff. They're probably not that good at hiding things anyway, I bet we find our outfits really easily. What's the time?'

'Twenty past eight,' I said, after taking my phone out of my pocket to check. 'We've got forty minutes. Let's hurry.'

So we searched EVERYWHERE we could think of, including our dorm, the classrooms, the corridors, the kitchen cupboards and the art room. We even barged into Cleo and Clarice's dorm and searched that, much to their amusement.

'Still haven't found your silly old outfits?' Clarice smiled. 'Time's running out girls, the mini bus is leaving in ten minutes.'

In desperation we put on our thick coats and went out to search the grounds. We looked in the stables, Bertie's shed, and the lockers and changing rooms in the swimming pool. As we came back out into the fresh air empty handed, Arabella said,

'What's that noise?'

We listened. It was the unmistakeable sound of the mini bus's engine, and it was getting fainter and fainter.

'They've gone,' I groaned, putting my hands to my head. 'I bet Cleo and Clarice told Bertie we are ill and can't come. I can't believe it. They're trying to ruin our Christmas.'

'Well we won't let them,' Arabella grabbed my hand and pulled hard. 'Come on, there's one last place we haven't looked.'

We arrived at the reindeers' shed to see the four animals standing peacefully side by side, munching hay. The door was open, Mr and Mrs Brandy-Snap must have just left because their water trough was full of fresh sparkling water and they all had Christmassy reindeer treats laid out in front of them.

'Merry Christmas reindeer,' I said glumly, not feeling at all Christmassy any longer.

'Davina, come here,' Arabella called from the back of the shed. 'Look what I've found.'

I walked over and saw her unrolling a pile of glittery clothes.

'I've found our Christmas outfits! Those idiots just threw them at the back of the reindeer shed. They are rather covered in straw but that's easy enough to brush off. Come on, give me a hand.'

We set to work and in minutes my hat, bracelets, scarf and legwarmers and Arabella's bobble hat and scarf looked good as new.

'Hang on, what's that?' My stomach did a flip as I spotted the folded piece of paper stuffed in the corner of the shed's window frame. My fingers shook as I unfolded it.

'"Well done, you made it, hip hip hurray.

A great success on Christmas Day.

Now hurry to the care home show,

Your prize is waiting there, so GO!"

'Well that's all very well, but how on earth are we going to get to Little Pineham Care Home?' Arabella asked. 'The minibus has gone and we'll never be able to walk there in time.'

'Aha,' I said, feeling mega excited. I patted a reindeer's back. 'I think I have a plan. If travelling with reindeer is good enough for Father Christmas, then it's good enough for us. Let's get our Christmas outfits on and jump on a reindeer each. It will probably be the same as riding a pony and I'm sure Mr and Mrs Brandy-Snap will understand, under the circumstances.'

'You're crazy,' Arabella grinned as she pulled on her

bobble hat and wound the scarf round her neck. 'But I like it. Come on then, there's no time to lose!'

I put on my hat, scarf, bracelets and legwarmers, then hoisted myself up onto the back of the calmest looking reindeer. Arabella went for the liveliest looking one and seconds later these lovely animals were walking across the school grounds with us on their backs!

Nobody stopped us or called out, after all everyone else was in Little Pineham and the Brandy-Snaps had probably gone back to their cottage to enjoy Christmas Day. Marcel and his chefs never went outside in winter if they could help it, preferring the cosiness of central heating.

'What about the cattle grids?' Arabella called, as a snowflake fluttered down and landed on one of my reindeer's antlers.

'We'll head towards the gate, I'll just hop down for a minute and open it,' I called back. 'Then I think we'll go cross-country towards Little Pineham, it will be quicker.'

My plan worked so wonderfully, that ten minutes later Arabella and I were galloping across fields with twirling snowflakes surrounding us. The landscape in front of us looked magical, the tops of trees and hedges slowly turning white as the snow began to settle. I could see the church spire in Little Pineham getting closer and closer as the reindeer galloped happily along, and the Christmassy feeling I'd lost so suddenly came back twice as strong.

It wasn't long before we slowed the reindeer down – it was just like riding rather short horses – and came out of the last field, up the track and into Little Pineham's high street. We knew the village quite well, because we are allowed to go shopping in groups of at least five every now and again, and Arabella said she thought the Elderly Care Home was up the hill past the police station, so that's the direction we headed.

There were a few people about, who stared at us in amazement, and we shouted "Merry Christmas" to them, and they shouted it back, and all in all it was a rather jolly journey.

Luckily Arabella was right about the direction of the Care Home, we spotted the school minibus outside so knew we'd come to the right place. We tied the reindeer up to a tree with a length of washing line attached to the side of the building, dusted the snow from our coats, hats and scarves, and pushed open the front door.

A cheery receptionist greeted us.

'Oh hello, you must be from Egmont School for Girls. Miss Fairchild said there might be two more arriving at some point. Come with me, they're just about to start.'

She started off down a corridor that had tinsel hanging round old black and white photographs that showed Little Pineham a hundred years ago, and we followed. She pushed open some double doors at the end and led us into a large room. Rows of chairs had been put out in a semi-circle and each had a beaming old lady or man on it. There were also several wheelchairs that made up the semicircle, and I almost fell over when I realised my old nanny, Carrie Whepple, was sitting in one of them!

'Cooeee Davina,' she called, waving at me. 'You made

it! I was getting a bit worried about you. This is Nora,' she pointed at a thin lady with long grey hair who was sitting on a chair next to her. Nora gave us a wave. 'She drove me over here so I could see you, bless her.'

'Ah Davina and Arabella, wonderful to see you,' Mrs Fairchild came over – still wearing her Mother Christmas outfit - and gestured for us to come and take our places with the rest of the Egmont Girls. 'What took you so long?'

'Cleo and Clarice hid our Christmassy outfits that we made yesterday with Nicola Nutmeg,' Arabella said loudly. 'By the time we found them chucked at the back of the reindeer shed, Bertie had driven everyone else off. We had to hitch rides on the backs of two reindeer to make it here in time. They're currently tied to a washing line outside.'

'Clarice told me you two was ill,' Bertie croaked from his chair in the semi-circle as gasped came from the assembled throng. 'She said you wasn't comin'.'

'Oh dear,' Mrs Fairchild turned grave eyes on Cleo and Clarice, who went red. 'In that case I'm sure the two girls in question will have a lovely time doing all the washing up in the care home kitchen after the carol concert and mince pies are finished.'

Cleo and Clarice looked horrified.

'Anyway,' Miss Fairchild gave a twirl then clapped her hands. 'Back to business.' We took our places next to Simone. 'I hope you enjoy the carols everybody.'

The concert went rather well.com, even though I do say so myself. The elderly men and women, including Carrie and Nora, sang along as we belted out the Christmas songs at the top of our voices. They even asked us for an encore so we sang We Wish You A Merry Christmas. Afterwards, Mrs Fairchild, who'd been conducting us all the way through, turned and said,

'We hope you enjoyed our concert and we wish you all a very merry Christmas. Now, the good staff here reliably inform me that if we all head towards the dining room there are some delicious Christmas treats and drinks awaiting us.'

As everyone else tumbled off towards the dining room, all chatting loudly except Cleo and Clarice, who walked at the back of the crowd, their shoulders drooping, Arabella and I made our way over to Carrie and Nora. Carrie sat beaming from her wheelchair, her ankle sticking out from under her skirt, all wrapped up in thick white plaster.

'Well done, girls,' she said as we approached. 'That was a lovely way to start Christmas morning, you've done your school proud.'

'But Carrie,' I said, my heart literally bursting because I

was so pleased to see her. 'I had no idea you were coming. I'm so glad, I missed seeing you over Christmas.'

'And I've missed you, Duckie,' Carrie said. 'Come and give your old nanny a hug.'

So I leant forwards and gave her the biggest bear hug EVER while Nora chatted to Arabella.

'Erm,' Carrie said, after I'd stood up again. 'Is us being here at the carol concert the only surprise you've had this Christmas, Davina?'

'No, someone sent me a Christmas card in code, and we – Hang on a minute! You know something about that don't you?'

'It was us!' Nora blurted out, before Carrie could say anything. 'Carrie told me what to write and I wrote the card and the clues. I knew that my handwriting would confuse you – it's quite shaky nowadays because of my arthritis. Your deputy head, Mr Portly, hid them before he went away on his holidays. Friend of my grandson's, lovely chap.'

'Wow,' Arabella breathed and Carrie and Nora blushed proudly. 'What an amazing plan. You certainly kept us on our toes.'

'Well I was so sorry not to be able to look after Davina over Christmas, I wanted to give her some sort of present that would keep you both busy so that you enjoyed your holidays at Egmont. And I know what great detectives you both are, so the idea just popped into my head one afternoon!'

'You're the absolute best, Carrie,' I said, throwing myself forwards to give her another bear hug.

'But that's not the end of the surprises,' Nora beamed. 'Go on, tell them Carrie.'

'Miss Fairchild, who's been in on the secret from the beginning, has given you both permission to come back to Nora's house for the rest of the day. Nora is a brilliant cook, aren't you old thing? And she's making a Christmas dinner with all the trimmings. Then we've got presents and party games to play.

That's your prize for finding all the clues!'

'Yippee,' Arabella and I shrieked at the same time. Miss Fairchild came waltzing over.

'I couldn't help overhearing,' she trilled. 'Aren't Carrie and Nora magnificent, girls? The way they planned the whole mystery for you! I hardly did anything, just had to throw you off the scent once at the beginning.'

'Yes they are,' I said, grinning at Carrie and her friend. 'This is turning out to be the best Christmas Day EVER!'

As we walked towards the door we could hear Cleo and Clarice banging cups and saucers around in the kitchen. Mrs

Pumpernickle was obviously giving them a lesson in washing up.

'Put the cup into the bubbles in the sink, dear. Goodness me, how do you think it's going to get clean unless you scrub it? I almost think you've never done any washing up before.'

'I haven't,' Cleo snapped. 'We have maids who do it at home.'

'Well in that case it's high time you learnt,' Mrs Pumpernickle said sharply.

Arabella and I grinned at each other and followed Nora, who was pushing Carrie and her wheelchair. Miss Fairchild had told us not to worry about the reindeer, that she'd already telephoned the Brandy-Snaps and they were bringing their special truck down to collect them.

Right, we're nearly at Nora's house now, Diary, so I've got to go. Nora drove us there in her groovy.com tiny car, me and Arabella are squashed in the back and Carrie and Nora are in the front. I can see twinkly Christmas lights through her windows, it looks magical in there and I can't wait for Christmas dinner, I'm absolutely STARVING.com. So I've only got one thing left to say:

MERRY CHRISTMAS.COM!

14124695R00060

Printed in Great Britain
by Amazon.co.uk, Ltd.,
Marston Gate.